Chester and Daisy move on

A story about two bear cubs who are adopted

Angela Lidster

BAAF
ADOPTION
& FOSTERING

Published by
British Association for Adoption & Fostering
(BAAF)
Skyline House
200 Union Street
London SE1 0LX
www.baaf.org.uk

© BAAF 1995
Reprinted 1999
Reprinted 2003

British Library Cataloguing in Publication Data

A catalogue reference record for this book is available from the British Library

ISBN 1 873868 19 7

Illustrations © Robyn Allpress
Designed by Between the Lines
Printed and bound by Russell Press (TU)

Chester and Daisy's birth family

Once upon a time there was a family of bears.
There was a mummy bear and a daddy bear and
two little bear cubs called Chester and Daisy. The
bear family lived in a little house with a red chimney,
a blue door and four small windows.

Your own page

Families are not all the same. Some families have one parent, some have two . . . some have one child, some have two, three or even more.

Some families live in houses or in flats or in caravans. Some share a house with other families and some travel around the country.

Tell me about **your birth family**. How is it different to Chester and Daisy's? Can you draw a picture of your birth family? Don't forget yourself of course!

The bear family used to live quite happily but after a while, mummy and daddy bear began to have a lot of arguments.

Chester and Daisy didn't know why mummy and daddy argued, but it made them feel very sad. Sometimes they felt so sad, they began to cry.

But mummy and daddy bear were so busy being cross with each other, they didn't notice how sad their little bear cubs had become.

Sometimes they shouted at Chester and Daisy just because they were crying, and that made Chester and Daisy feel even more unhappy.

Chester and Daisy loved their mummy and daddy but they began to think that their mummy and daddy didn't love them. That wasn't true of course… it was just that mummy and daddy bear had stopped loving each other and they forgot to tell their little bear cubs that they still loved them.

One day, daddy bear decided to leave the little house with the red chimney, the blue door and the four small windows.

Chester and Daisy missed daddy bear, and they began to wonder if it was their fault that he had gone away.

Sometimes daddy bear sent Chester and Daisy picture postcards, and he wrote 'love from daddy bear' with lots of kisses... so Chester and Daisy knew that daddy bear still loved them.

Your own page

Chester and Daisy felt sad when their mummy and daddy argued and they felt happy when daddy bear sent them picture postcards.

What makes **you** feel sad? And what makes **you** feel happy? Can you draw sad and happy faces?

Mummy bear found it hard to manage all by herself and she began to feel more and more unhappy.

Chester and Daisy tried to cheer her up. They tried to be very good and they helped around the house and they sang songs they had learned at nursery school!

But mummy bear didn't cheer up. Sometimes she shouted at Chester and Daisy because they made too much noise when they played, or because they chattered instead of eating their dinner. She forgot that it's hard for little bear cubs to be perfectly good all the time.

Sometimes mummy bear felt too tired to get their dinner ready so Chester and Daisy were hungry.

One day the doctor came to see mummy bear and she said that she was very poorly and should be looked after in the hospital. The doctor told the social worker all about it, and the social worker said that the little bear cubs could be looked after by a foster bear family until their mummy was better.

Chester and Daisy were quite worried about going to live with a new bear family because it would feel very strange living in someone else's house. Chester and Daisy wondered what their foster bear family had for breakfast... would they know that **their** favourite breakfast was porridge and honey?

Your own page

Chester and Daisy thought it would be very strange living in someone else's house.

What did **you** think about when you were moving to live with your foster family?

Chester and Daisy move to a foster bear family

Chester and Daisy found that some things were different. Their foster bear family lived in a bigger house which didn't have a blue door, and there were lots more bears to look after them... a mummy bear, three grown up bear cubs, and a grandma and grandpa bear. There was also another baby bear cub living with the foster bear family for a while, just like Chester and Daisy.

But they found some things were just the same. The foster bear family ate porridge and honey for breakfast and they liked to sing nursery school songs! The foster bear family had to learn a lot about Chester and Daisy, but they did their best to make Chester and Daisy feel at home.

Soon Chester and Daisy felt very safe and happy. They still loved their mummy and daddy and they missed them, but they began to love their foster bear family too. And what's more, their foster bear family loved them back!

That made Chester and Daisy feel all warm and snugly inside... just like cuddling a hot water bottle on a cold winter night!!

Your own page

Foster families are not all the same.

Tell me about **your** foster family. Can you draw a picture of them? And don't forget to draw yourself!

Adoption means belonging

After a while, the social worker went to see Chester and Daisy because she had something very important to tell them. The social worker knew that it was very hard for little bear cubs to understand, but she tried her best to explain what had happened to their mummy and daddy, and what would happen next.

The social worker told Chester and Daisy that she had written to daddy bear to tell him where they were living so he could still send them picture postcards. Daddy bear had told her all about his new job travelling around the country and how much he liked it. He told her that he could not take Chester and Daisy with him, and that he could not come home again because he and mummy bear would not be happy, and if they were unhappy Chester and Daisy would be too.

The social worker told Chester and Daisy that she had seen mummy bear to tell her about daddy bear. Mummy bear had told her that even though she was getting better, it was too hard for her to be a mummy bear and that she could not look after Chester and Daisy properly.

Now little bear cubs need someone to look after them properly, as well as to love them, so they can grow up to be well and strong and happy. Mummy bear couldn't do that for Chester and Daisy, and daddy bear had gone away, so they needed to live with a mummy and daddy who would love them and look after them forever.

The social worker used a word that Chester and Daisy had never heard before – '**adoption**'. They wondered what it meant, so she explained that it meant having a new family and '**belonging**'. She said it was a very special thing to happen to two very special bear cubs.

Your own page

It must have been hard for Chester and Daisy to think about why they could not live with their mummy and daddy.

It must be hard for you too but can **you** tell me something that happened in your birth family that means you can't live with them?

Chester and Daisy feel muddled

At first, Chester and Daisy thought **adoption** might be a good idea, but then they began to think it might not be.

'Our foster bear family love us and look after us properly,' they said. 'Why can't we stay with them?'

The social worker explained to Chester and Daisy that a foster bear family look after little bear cubs for some time, but they do not grow up **belonging** as they do in an adoptive bear family.

Chester and Daisy felt all muddled up inside.

They felt **happy** about having a new family, but they felt **sad** about leaving their foster bear family, because it's always sad to say goodbye to someone you love.

They felt **excited** about all the new things they were going to do, but they also felt **scared** about all the new things!!

They felt **pleased** that they would have a new family to belong to, but they felt **angry** that their mummy and daddy could not look after them.

They felt **worried** that their new mummy and daddy wouldn't know that they liked porridge and honey for breakfast... but they felt quite **sure** that they would find out just like their foster bear family did.

Sometimes, Chester and Daisy didn't feel worried at all.

But at other times they felt so muddled up it made their tummies ache just like when they'd eaten too much porridge and honey! Ugh! it felt YUKKY!!!!

Sometimes, all the muddled up feelings inside made Chester and Daisy feel quite cross and grumpy. Sometimes their foster bear family felt cross and grumpy too, because it seemed that Chester and Daisy were cross and grumpy for no good reason at all. But really, it was because they had so much to think about, and that's a hard thing for little bear cubs to do.

Your own page

Chester and Daisy made funny faces to show their feelings.

What muddled up feelings do **you** have? Sit in front of a mirror and make your face show how you feel. Can you draw a picture of how your face looks in the mirror?

The social worker talked to Chester and Daisy and to their foster bear family, and she explained that it was OK to feel that way sometimes.

She also told them about a very good special secret. She told them that all little bear cubs are filled with love inside, and that they have so much love, they have plenty to give to everyone.

They have enough love to give to their foster bear family...

and enough love to give their mummy and daddy bear...

and enough love to give to each other...

and enough love to give to their adoptive family...

And the reason they have so much love to give is because **so many** people loved them, and that made their love grow and GROW and GROW...

'So remember little bear cubs,' said the social worker, 'even when you go to live with your new adoptive bear family, your foster bear family will still love you, and your mummy and daddy will still love you, and it's OK for you to love them.'

That was a very good secret… and one which the little bear cubs could share!

Your own page

See if you can draw all the people **you** love!

Chester and Daisy's important news

One day, the social worker came along to tell Chester and Daisy some news. She had found an adoptive mummy and daddy who were just right for Chester and Daisy.

She showed them some photos of their new mummy and daddy and told them about where they lived and what they liked to do.

Chester and Daisy's new mummy and daddy visited them and soon they all got to know each other.

Chester and Daisy liked their new mummy and daddy very much, but they still felt a little scared about going to live with them.

Your own page

Chester and Daisy felt a little scared about going to live with their new mummy and daddy.

What do **you** think it will be like living with your adoptive family? Can you draw a picture of them?

But before that could happen, Chester and Daisy had something special to do... they said goodbye to their mummy and daddy.

It was a sad time because it's always sad to say goodbye to someone you love. Mummy and daddy bear told Chester and Daisy that they wanted them to be happy and to grow up belonging to their new family. The social worker took photos and promised to send one to everyone.

Then she explained that after Chester and Daisy were living with their new family, mummy bear would write letters so they would know how she was, and daddy bear would send picture postcards to show the places he travelled to... and Chester and Daisy would send school photos so their mummy and daddy would be able to see them growing up.

Your own page

Chester and Daisy were able to say goodbye to their mummy and daddy, and keep in touch after they moved to their adoptive family.

Do you think **you** might be able to have a goodbye visit with your mummy or daddy? Who else in your birth family would you like to see, or keep in touch with, when it's time for you to be adopted?

Chester and Daisy move on

One bright sunny morning, Chester and Daisy were helped by their foster bear family to pack the last of their clothes and toys because it was time to move to their adoptive bear family. They had already taken quite a lot of things to their new home, but there was still a suitcase, two boxes and a bike to get into the little car… as well as Chester and Daisy and their adoptive mummy and daddy! What a squash!

It was quite hard for Chester and Daisy and their foster bear family to say goodbye to each other, and everyone felt a bit sad.

But they also felt happy, because Chester and Daisy were going to be **adopted** by a mummy and daddy who would love them and look after them, even when they were grown up.

And after a while, Chester and Daisy realised something very special...

Instead of having all the muddled up feelings inside which gave them an ache in their tummy, they felt all warm and snugly, because they were loved and cared for, and...

they were very happy little bear cubs.